*Acting Edition*

I0740967

# Mother Play

## A Play in Five Evictions

by Paula Vogel

Copyright © 2024 by Paula Vogel
All Rights Reserved

*MOTHER PLAY* is fully protected under the copyright laws of the United States of America, the British Commonwealth, including Canada, and all member countries of the Berne Convention for the Protection of Literary and Artistic Works, the Universal Copyright Convention, and/ or the World Trade Organization conforming to the Agreement on Trade Related Aspects of Intellectual Property Rights. All rights, including professional and amateur stage productions, recitation, lecturing, public reading, motion picture, radio broadcasting, television, online/digital production, and the rights of translation into foreign languages are strictly reserved.

ISBN 978-0-573-71141-1

www.concordtheatricals.com
www.concordtheatricals.co.uk

**FOR PRODUCTION INQUIRIES**

UNITED STATES AND CANADA
info@concordtheatricals.com
1-866-979-0447

UNITED KINGDOM AND EUROPE
licensing@concordtheatricals.co.uk
020-7054-7298

Each title is subject to availability from Concord Theatricals Corp., depending upon country of performance. Please be aware that *MOTHER PLAY* may not be licensed by Concord Theatricals Corp. in your territory. Professional and amateur producers should contact the nearest Concord Theatricals Corp. office or licensing partner to verify availability.

CAUTION: Professional and amateur producers are hereby warned that *MOTHER PLAY* is subject to a licensing fee. The purchase, renting, lending or use of this book does not constitute a license to perform this title(s), which license must be obtained from Concord Theatricals Corp. prior to any performance. Performance of this title(s) without a license is a violation of federal law and may subject the producer and/or presenter of such performances to civil penalties. Both amateurs and professionals considering a production are strongly advised to apply to the appropriate agent before starting rehearsals, advertising, or booking a theatre. A licensing fee must be paid whether the title(s) is presented for charity or gain and whether or not admission is charged. Professional/Stock licensing fees are quoted upon application to Concord Theatricals Corp.

This work is published by Samuel French, an imprint of Concord Theatricals Corp.

No one shall make any changes in this title(s) for the purpose of production. No part of this book may be reproduced, stored in a retrieval system, scanned, uploaded, or transmitted in any form, by any means, now known or yet to be invented, including mechanical, electronic, digital, photocopying, recording, videotaping, or otherwise, without the prior written permission of the publisher. No one shall share this title(s), or any part of this title(s), through any social media or file hosting websites.

For all inquiries regarding motion picture, television, online/digital and other media rights, please contact Jonathan Lomma at WME Agency, 11 Madison Avenue, 18th Floor, New York, NY 10010. Email: JDL@ WMEAgency.com

## MUSIC AND THIRD-PARTY MATERIALS USE NOTE

Licensees are solely responsible for obtaining formal written permission from copyright owners to use copyrighted music and/or other copyrighted third-party materials (e.g. artworks, logos) in the performance of this play and are strongly cautioned to do so. If no such permission is obtained by the licensee, then the licensee must use only original music and materials that the licensee owns and controls. Licensees are solely responsible and liable for clearances of all third-party copyrighted materials, including without limitation music, and shall indemnify the copyright owners of the play(s) and their licensing agent, Concord Theatricals Corp., against any costs, expenses, losses and liabilities arising from the use of such copyrighted third-party materials by licensees. For music, please contact the appropriate music licensing authority in your territory for the rights to any incidental music.

## IMPORTANT BILLING AND CREDIT REQUIREMENTS

If you have obtained performance rights to this title, please refer to your licensing agreement for important billing and credit requirements.

*MOTHER PLAY* was first produced by Second Stage Theater (Carole Rothman, President & Artistic Director; Lisa Lawer Post, Executive Director) and premiered at the Helen Hayes Theater on April 25, 2024. The performance was directed by Tina Landau, with scenic design by David Zinn, costume design by Toni-Leslie James, lighting design by Jen Schriever, sound design by Jill BC Du Boff, and projection design by Shawn Duan. The production stage manager was John C. Moore. The cast was as follows:

**PHYLLIS HERMAN** . . . . . . . . . . . . . . . . . . . . . . . . . . . . . . . . . Jessica Lange
**CARL HERMAN** . . . . . . . . . . . . . . . . . . . . . . . . . . . . . . . . . . . . . Jim Parsons
**MARTHA HERMAN** . . . . . . . . . . . . . . . . . . . . . . . . . . . Celia Keenan-Bolger

# CHARACTERS

**PHYLLIS HERMAN** – The Mother. Ages 30s to late 70s/80s.
**CARL HERMAN** – The Son. Ages 13–37. The genius in the family.
**MARTHA HERMAN** – The Daughter. Ages 11–50s.

# SETTING

A series of apartments. In the beginning of the play, these apartments are the custodial units, sub-basement, in what we now call Section 8 housing.

# TIME

From 1964 into 21st-century America.

# AUTHOR'S NOTES

**By the way:** this play is not naturalistic. The walls may or may not meet. But since it is a memory play, even the cockroaches have a touch of magic.

Music. And muzak.

**A note about cockroaches:** please be playful. At the Helen Hayes Theatre, the production used projections. I ask you to make a story when the roaches dance in transitions. A salute to Hollywood dance legends, or an Ethel Williams homage with roaches in the toilet, etc. For now, I am simply suggesting a courtship story: the roaches court their mates through dance, followed by marriage, followed by hundreds of baby roaches. But you choose!

**About the purse:** it is magical. The way our mothers' purses are when we are toddlers: the purse can hold infinity. Please sprinkle some magic throughout these basement apartments. Phyllis pulls props out of her purse that – by the laws of physics – should not be able to fit.

# NOTE ON SONGS

The original Broadway production of *Mother Play* used the following songs. Permission to include these songs in a production is <u>not</u> included with a license from Concord Theatricals. If any licensee wishes to use any or all of these songs in their production of *Mother Play*, they must acquire the necessary rights from the applicable music publishers.

| | |
|---|---|
| "So What's New?" | "Baker Street" |
| "Mercy Mercy" | "Un Cellier" |
| "Because" | "Disco Inferno" |
| "Do Wah Diddy Diddy" | "I Will Survive" |
| "There's a Small Hotel" | "I Will Wait for You" |
| "Moon River" | "In the Mood" |
| "Stranger on the Shore" | "The Way You Look Tonight" |
| "Pavane pour une infante défunte" | "My Romance" |
| "La Cucaracha" | "Harmelodial Introduction" |
| "My Blue Heaven" | "Perpetuum Mobile" |
| "The Fashion Show" | "Pie Jesu" |
| "There's No You" | "Dance of the Blessed Spirits" |
| "Theme from *A Summer Place*" | "La Vergine degli Angeli" |
| "Lullaby" | "Jeanie with the Light Brown Hair" |
| "Work Song" | |
| "Ride of the Valkyries" | "Steal Away" |
| "You've Lost That Lovin' Feelin'" | "Nearer, My God, to Thee" |
| "Soul Finger" | "My Foolish Heart" |
| "Classical Gas" | "The More I See You" |

# NOTE ON MUSIC & IMAGES

A license to produce *Mother Play* does not include a performance license for any third-party or copyrighted music or recordings, or publicly display any branded logos or trademarked images. For indicated music cues on the pages listed below, licensees should acquire the necessary rights to use an existing song, create an original composition, or use music in the public domain.

Page 2 – "1960s music"

Page 6 – "a rock and roll song from 1960–64 with inane lyrics"; "the easy listening station"

Page 7 – "an instrumental standard"

Page 13 – "music"

Page 28 – "a snippet from a musical torch song."

Page 38 – "A 1970s disco song"; "a beloved 1970s disco tune"

Page 39 – "another disco anthem"

Page 42 – "a medley of soft and easy music"

Page 43 – "Rodgers and Hammerstein, Porter, Gershwin, a sprinkle of hits"

Page 54 – "Fauré's 'Pie Jesu'"; "Gluck's 'Dance of the Blessed Spirits'"; "La Vergine degli Angeli"; "I Dream of Jeanie"; "Steal Away"; "Nearer My God to Thee"; "Easy soft listening music"

Page 57 – "The standard song, Phyllis' favorite"

For trademarked images indicated on the pages listed below, licensees must acquire rights for any logos and/or images or create their own.

Page 5 – "a large McDonald's bag"

Page 44 – "Tabasco"

For further information, please see the Music and Third-Party Materials Use Note on page iii.

*MOTHER PLAY, A Play in Five Evictions, is dedicated to Mark Vogel.*

## Present Moment in Time

(**MARTHA** *enters the stage. In the middle of the stage there is a sealed moving box.*)

**MARTHA.** After I left my mother's house, I worked for a time as a packer in a moving van company. In Washington, D.C. people are always moving. Republicans in, Democrats out. Democrats in, Republicans. Out.

By age eleven, I had already moved seven times. My father had a habit of not paying rent. My mother, brother and I could pack up our house in a day.

A very useful skill. To know what household goods are in every box so one can also unpack in a day. Family in, family out.

When I packed up my brother Carl's apartment after he died, everything he left behind fit into one medium size U-Haul box.

There is a season for packing. And a season for unpacking.

(**MARTHA** *pulls out a box cutter and slices through the taped box. She pulls out a stuffed rabbit, a book –)*

(– **CARL** *begins to appear –)*

(– *and finally a piece of paper, which she reads from.*)

"Dear Martha"

(**CARL** *is now fully present, in the past, and as music rises,* **MARTHA** *goes to him. Together they begin moving furniture and boxes into the space.)*

*(Once all the furniture pieces are in place,* **MARTHA** *goes into the hall and pushes in a big knockoff Eames lounge chair. When the chair is in the living room,* **MARTHA** *turns it. There in the chair is* **PHYLLIS**. *In her lap is a huge purse.)*

**MARTHA**.   ERIE STREET, ADELPHI MARYLAND. BASEMENT APARTMENT. 1964. MARTHA 12, CARL 14. PHYLLIS 37.

*(The apartment at Erie Street comes to life. A two-bedroom apartment built in the 1940s. Ugly ceiling fixtures. The metal door into the hallway is open. There is a flight down from the front door.)*

*(A sofa. Two armchairs. A round walnut coffee table. Lamps, a rug. Knockoff Scandinavian furniture. Earth colors. There is a dim light from the living room window coming from ground windows halfway up the wall. The apartment is the custodial unit.)*

*(***MARTHA*** takes out a radio and turns it on – 1960s music. The siblings smile at each other.)*

*(As* **MARTHA** *and* **CARL** *unpack boxes,* **PHYLLIS**, *in a daze, watches her* **CHILDREN** *work.)*

Is it all going to fit?

**CARL.** Anything that doesn't fit goes on the street. Someone will take it.

**MARTHA.** Okay.

> (**PHYLLIS** *takes her cigarettes out of her purse. Sits. Then she searches her purse. Finds the ashtray in her purse. Sits. Then starts looking in her purse. Looking. Looking.*)

**PHYLLIS.** God Damn It.

**CARL.** What.

**PHYLLIS.** My lighter.

**CARL.** It's...somewhere.

**PHYLLIS.** It's a gift from Sonny.

**CARL.** You didn't leave it behind.

**PHYLLIS.** Engraved. The only boy I ever loved.

**CARL.** What about the other four boys?

**MARTHA.** It will show up.

> (**CARL** *roots in his pocket and brings out matches. Goes to his* **MOTHER**'s *chair and lights her cigarette.* **PHYLLIS** *breathes it in as if it is oxygen on a planet without air. She exhales. Breathes. Less shaky now.* **PHYLLIS** *calms.*)

**PHYLLIS.** Thanks, love.

> (**PHYLLIS** *goes back on the hunt in her purse. She pulls out a small bottle of gin.*)

Martha, love...where did we put the –

> (**MARTHA** *opens another box. Pulls out a high glass. Hands it to her* **MOTHER**.)

**PHYLLIS**.  I need ice.

> (**MARTHA** *opens another box. Pulls out an old-fashioned metal ice cube tray. Cranks it. Hands it to* **CARL**. **CARL** *puts three ice cubes into Phyllis' glass. Clink.* **PHYLLIS** *pours a stiff shot of gin. Swirls her glass. Then puts the glass to her mouth. Her* **CHILDREN** *watch.* **PHYLLIS** *savors the gin. Ahhh. Her brain chemistry changes.*)

Mother just might get through this.

> (**MARTHA** *opens up a new box. It's her mother's lingerie.*)

**MARTHA**.  Should I put your underwear on the bed?

**PHYLLIS**.  Carl will know where everything goes. He's gone through my private things at least every week since he was four years old.

**CARL**.  I am not the slightest bit interested in your underwear.

**PHYLLIS**.  (*A silent laugh, an exhale of smoke.*) Just put it on the bed. I'll put it away.

> (**MARTHA** *lifts up the box, exits, and reenters.*)

**CARL**.  You caught me just once.

I was searching for money.

**PHYLLIS**.  Right.

> (*With the move in mostly complete, both* **KIDS** *throw themselves on the furniture.* **CARL** *whips out a book and buries himself in it. All of his life,* **CARL** *can read while talking and hearing every word.*)

**CARL**.  What's for dinner.

**PHYLLIS.** Shit on a shingle what's it to you.

(Her **CHILDREN** are relieved to hear the old
**PHYLLIS**.)

**CARL.** Well, mother, you haven't lost your way with words
in the move.

(**PHYLLIS** takes one last puff and stubs out the
cigarette in her ashtray. Then she dives into
her purse and pulls out a large McDonald's
bag.)

**PHYLLIS.** Ta da!

**MARTHA.** Really?!

(She distributes the burgers to her **CHILDREN**.
Puts the fries carefully on napkins on the
coffee table.)

**CARL.** One day scientists will discover Amelia Earhart's
plane in the bottom of your purse. What else are you
hiding from us in there?

**PHYLLIS.** Everything but money.

This meal is the last of my spending cash this week.
You should know that when your father abandoned us,
he also cleared out our checking and saving accounts.

**MARTHA.** You mean this is the last hamburger we can buy?

**PHYLLIS.** Until we get back on our feet.

(**CARL** ritualistically eats his fries as if it's
his last meal; **MARTHA** slows her chewing.)

For school lunch, you'll make your own sandwiches –
there's bread and Velveeta cheese. For dinner, you'll set
the table, Martha, make the rice, and we'll heat up our
meal when I get home.

**MARTHA.** Why can't Carl make dinner? Set the table?

**PHYLLIS.** Your brother will be in the school library. On the Debate Team! 790 on his pre-SATs in English!

**MARTHA.** 480 in math.

**PHYLLIS.** Screw math. If your brother keeps it up, he is going to get a free ride to a good school. Somebody in this family will get a college degree.

   *(The radio plays a rock and roll song from 1960–64 with inane lyrics.* **MARTHA,** *enthused, leaps up and turns up the volume.)*

– Turn that noise down.

   (**MARTHA** *turns down the volume.)*

That's not music. (**PHYLLIS** *quotes an inane lyric.)* Those are lyrics?! The Gershwins wrote lyrics. Cole Porter – those are lyrics. Put my station on.

   (**MARTHA** *turns the dial to the easy listening station.)*

**CARL.** Your music has no lyrics at all.

**PHYLLIS.** *(Tapping her head.)* In here – all the lyrics.

**CARL.** They play this station in the psych ward of hospitals as they pass out sedation to the patients. They strap the inmates down and put mouth guards between their teeth. And then they'll hike up the volume and hike up the juice. *(Beat.)* Your music makes me want to slash my wrists.

**PHYLLIS.** What are you reading?

**CARL.** *One Flew Over the Cuckoo's Nest.*

**PHYLLIS.** – Martha, have you unpacked the knives yet? Your brother needs to slash his wrists.

**CARL.** I can't even jump out the window to end it all. You have to jump up half a story to reach the ground.

(**CARL** *fiddles with his now cold fries.*)

PHYLLIS.  *(Stung.)* This is the only apartment I could afford to rent! The custodial apartment is twenty bucks cheaper. All you have to do, son, is take the trash cans out once a week. Make yourself useful.

I owe my father the advance for the rent. And we are not going to the movies, to McDonald's, or to buy sodas until your grandfather is paid back every penny. Do you have any idea how hard it is to find work for a woman my age? I'm lucky I found a government typist job. You two have been living a life of ease: your sister had her own bedroom for two years. Tonight Martha moves into my bedroom.

(**MARTHA** *tries not to cry.*)

MARTHA.  You snore.

PHYLLIS.  Deal with it. You will learn to sleep to it like it's muzak.

(*The radio starts to play an instrumental standard.*)

I love this song. Turn it up.

(**MARTHA** *does so. An instrumental washes over the living room.* **CARL** *turns the volume down.*)

CARL.  Why don't we listen to the classical music station.

PHYLLIS.  You get to choose the radio stations when you are paying your share of rent.

CARL.  When I can afford the rent I will be at the Algonquin... Room Service. Elevators with elevator men. One of the seats at the Round Table waiting for me. The bartender knows what I drink. The cat comes out for a chin rub when she hears me at check-in.

**CARL**.  Or perhaps I will check into small pensiones in Italy on quiet cobblestoned streets away from the hubbub of American tourists.

Or perhaps –

**PHYLLIS**.  – Did you go to the wrong hospital when you were born?

**CARL**.  My being here is all a clerical mistake. I am the lost Romanov. Anastasia.

**PHYLLIS**.  When you come into your millions, all I ask is a small townhouse. A box at the National Theater. Oh and if you might pick up one small Fabergé Egg for your Mama for her étagère as a Christmas gift…

**MARTHA**.  I wanna room with Carl.

**PHYLLIS**.  "I wanna"? It's "I want to room." "I wanna." You will enunciate please.

I assume you know where to catch the bus on Monday?

**MARTHA**.  My class is studying what we studied in fourth grade.

**PHYLLIS**.  Great. You'll ace the exams. And next year, Martha, you will be in Junior High and old enough to take the typing classes.

**MARTHA**.  Why doesn't anyone care if Carl can type?

**PHYLLIS**.  Because you are going to be able to take care of yourself if and when your husband walks out on you with little mouths to feed. When your husband empties out your joint bank account and you find out he's keeping his mistress in a high rise in Georgetown. Besides, Carl will be typing. His first novel. His work that he will dedicate to his mother.

> (**PHYLLIS** *goes digging in her purse and comes out with two latch keys.)*

Here – put these around your neck when you leave the house. You are to come straight home when the school bus lets you off. I can't afford to lose this job so you are on your own if your mouth gets you in trouble. I am talking to you, Mr. Herman.

> (**MARTHA** *and* **CARL** *solemnly take their latch key.*)

Well, my little loves. Today is the day our lives get better. We will look back and discover what great good fortune it was when that son of a bitch – your father – walked out on us. No matter what, I have you two. I'm lucky to be so close to my children.

> (**MARTHA** *and* **CARL** *are quiet.* **PHYLLIS** *kisses her* **SON**'s *cheek ardently and pats/air kisses* **MARTHA**.*)

**MARTHA**. Good night.

**CARL**. Sleep tight!

> (**PHYLLIS** *leaves. The two* **SIBLINGS** *look at each other.*)

**MARTHA**. I'm sleeping on the sofa.

**CARL**. She will get pissed.

> (**MARTHA** *goes to a box in the corner. She opens it and takes out stuffed animals. We see the stuffed Rabbit.*)

I don't want our old stuffed animals.

**MARTHA**. Neither do I. I don't know why she insisted on packing them. We'll put them on the curb. Kids will take them.

**CARL**. It's over, isn't it?

**MARTHA**. What?

**CARL.** Childhood.

> (*In answer,* **MARTHA** *takes up the box, and* **CARL** *opens the front door.* **MARTHA** *decides to save the stuffed Rabbit.*)

## Transition – Outside the Trash Room

> (*In the break,* **CARL** *struggles with the trash cans up the stairs. He drops the can he is carrying, and manically brushes his clothes off from the roaches. Stomps. Shudders. Food that has been rotting for a week in the Maryland heat. Takes a deep breath, and as quickly as he can, carries the brimming can up the stairs.*)

## Afterschool Erie Street, 1964

> (**CARL** *is on the knockoff Eames chair reading. He hears someone struggling at the door. Then a pounding. He jumps up.*)

> (**MARTHA** *enters. Breathless. Her tight t-shirt has been ripped. Her hair is a mess.*)

**CARL.** Why didn't you –

> (*He sees* **MARTHA**.)

**MARTHA.** I Am So Fucking Mad!

**CARL.** Martha?!

**MARTHA.** Mom's not home –? (*She is starting to cry.*)

**CARL.** Jesus What Happened? Are you –

**MARTHA.** – I have to change my shirt –

*(She starts to rush off.)*

**CARL.**  What happened?

*(**MARTHA** shakes her head no.)*

Tell me.

**MARTHA.**  There's this – fifteen-year-old boy on the bus. He's been held back twice in sixth grade. And he – usually just, ya know, makes kissing noises at me or yells out piggy things –

> *(She stops. She fingers her neck where the latchkey chain has rubbed her skin into a burn.)*

**CARL.**  What kind of things does this ruffian say?

**MARTHA.**  He says he can smell fish when he passes me and all the boys laugh. Even some of the girls.

**CARL.**  I hate boys.

**MARTHA.**  So I usually sit up front near the driver, but today there were no seats. I got hemmed into the middle of the aisle. And one boy behind me held me by my latch key chain, and the big guy started rubbing himself on me, and then he lifted my blouse and I started screaming but the girls got quiet and the boys were just – wild – And I yelled at the driver Help Me – but he just adjusted the mirror to watch, and then the boy ripped my top and –

I WANT TO BE A SIX-FOOT-TALL MAN! JUST LET ME BE A SIX-FOOT-TALL MAN for five Goddamn Minutes!

> *(**MARTHA** starts to cry. **CARL** awkwardly pats her shoulder.)*

**CARL.**  Martha. Sweetie. *(He gives her a tissue.)* I will go with you to the bus stop tomorrow.

**MARTHA.**  No. You won't. You are of more use to me alive. Don't tell Mother.

**CARL.**  No. I think not. Wait a moment.

>  (**CARL** *disappears and returns with one of his shirts. He puts it over her t-shirt.*)

Wear my shirt. Take my pants.

Dress as if you were going to an all-girl academy. Very Butch.

**MARTHA.**  Butch?

**CARL.**  You look good in my shirt. Keep it. Now –

>  (*He takes* **MARTHA**'*s hands.*)

Stand up. I want you to walk across the living room for me.

>  (**MARTHA** *does so.*)

Now walk back.

>  (*He watches.*)

You are using your hips. I want you to walk urgently but with command like Napoleon when he has to take a piss. Look:

>  (**CARL** *does a very aggressive walk.*)

Now you try:

>  (**MARTHA** *does.*)

You are slumping. It makes you look weak. Stand absolutely straight.

**MARTHA.**  But then my breasts are –

**CARL.**  You are to think that your breasts are a pair of gatling guns that will mow down any male stupid enough to try you – again!

*(**MARTHA** executes an almost martial walk quickly.)*

Perfection!

## Phyllis On the Runway, 1964

*(Fabulous lights; music; we could be watching the new Chanel collection in Milan.*

*(**PHYLLIS** stands triumphantly in a Chanel suit, and saunters down and back with Panache; then the lights turn into the ugly living room overhead lights, and the music turns to muzak.)*

**PHYLLIS.**  Look what I found! At Next to New! They have late hours on Friday night. Guess what designer this is!

**MARTHA.**  Salvation Army?

**PHYLLIS.**  No! Guess!

*(**CARL** looks up from his book.)*

**CARL.**  Givenchy.

**PHYLLIS.**  Close! Martha?

**MARTHA.**  I don't know.

**CARL.**  Dior.

**PHYLLIS.**  No.

*(**PHYLLIS** does another turn.)*

**CARL.**  Balenciaga.

*(No.)*

Pierre Cardin.

**PHYLLIS.**  Why do you know so many designers?

*(**MARTHA** cuts off her **MOTHER**'s diatribe.)*

**MARTHA.**  – So which designer?

**PHYLLIS.**  – Chanel! The woman had just rolled up in her Mercedes, and I practically ripped the suit out of her hand.

– guess how much I paid!

**MARTHA.**  I don't know.

**CARL.**  I thought every penny was going into the piggy bank to repay –

**PHYLLIS.**  – That Georgetown matron shelled out at least 100 dollars last year in Saks. Guess how much.

**MARTHA.**  Forty bucks.

**PHYLLIS.**  Nope.

**MARTHA.**  Thirty.

**PHYLLIS.**  Hah! Ten bucks!

**CARL.**  Why would a Georgetown matron bother to sell her clothes for ten dollars?

**PHYLLIS.**   Thrift stores aren't about secretaries and waitresses being thrifty – it's about the rich pinching their pennies. That's why they're rich. They're thrifty.

**CARL.**  No mother. This Potomac matron took her haute couture to a Capitol Hill reception so she could ornament her bureaucratic husband. And she tried to look elegant in the D.C. humidity until her haute couture is sweat-drenched. She smiles as the stockings trickle sweat into her high heels and she can feel the blisters forming. And her Saks Fifth Avenue Chanel now revolts her: she can still smell her sweat under the copious Arpège perfume and now the perfume revolts her too. And so she rushes home to peel the expensive wilting clothing off. She hands the limp Chanel to her maid for dry cleaning, and when she removes the plastic wrap she lifts the garment up to her face – and she can still, she imagines, smell her sweat. Smell the faint perfume. If she takes a deeper breath, she could swear that she smells the fetid canal water drifting from Georgetown that always makes her gag in August. And she only wore it once! And so she decides that some woman who works in the typing pool for the postal service can wear her high season sweat.

**PHYLLIS**. When did you get so angry? You, Mr. Herman, are becoming a radical. It is not becoming. You had better get rich on your writing so that you can buy your Mama Chanel hot off the racks in Saks Fifth Avenue.

You know, Martha, you should come with me next Sunday and find something a little more presentable with your babysitting money. Look at you! You are dressing like some – like a – like a –

**MARTHA**.  – like my brother?

**PHYLLIS**.  Like your father. You are the spitting image. Stand up young lady. You walk like a man. Now watch your mother.

This is how a woman walks:

> (**PHYLLIS** *demonstrates.*)

Now you.

> (**MARTHA** *still walks like Napoleon but with a strange hip sway that she saw her* **MOTHER** *do.*)

Oh dear God. Again: watch:

> (*And now* **PHYLLIS** *strolls in an even more exaggerated fashion – a cross between a prostitute and a drag queen.*)

> (**MARTHA** *tries and just can't.* **PHYLLIS** *laughs.*)

**MARTHA.**  I walk the way I walk because I want to get somewhere fast!

**PHYLLIS.**  I needed a good laugh. I am on my way to retire.

**CARL.**  Martha kept a plate warm for you in the oven.

**PHYLLIS.**  Thanks, love. I ate at the bar. Good night, children.

>   (**CARL** *sits stock still; both of them listen for the closing of the bedroom door.*)

>   (*Then –*)

## Another Fashion Show

>   (**CARL** *jumps up. Lights change back into the Milan runway, and* **CARL** *sashays and poses up and down the runway. He does a much better job than* **PHYLLIS** *did.* **MARTHA** *joins him on the runway: Napoleonic style with her gatling gun breasts ablaze.*)

**MARTHA.**  TWO YEARS LATER

>   (*The kitchen table. Late at night.* **MARTHA** *is writing a book report.* **CARL** *enters tentatively.*)

She's out. You can tap dance next to the bed and she won't hear you.

**CARL.**  – book report?

**MARTHA.**  Yes.

**CARL.**  For Miss Peggy Baldwin?

**MARTHA.**  Yes.

**CARL.**  She's sex starved.

**MARTHA.**  I don't want to think about Mrs. Baldwin in bed.

**CARL.** All troubles begin with sexual repression. Remember these words.

**MARTHA.** Don't you have homework?

**CARL.** Ridiculously easy. Finished it so I could read French history. Louis XIV. The Sun King.

Did you know that the gentlemen of Versailles considered it rude to knock upon a chamber door? Only a peasant would do so.

**MARTHA.** Mmhhm.

**CARL.** Gentlemen of the court developed long pinky fingernails and would scratch the door for admittance. Three times like so.

**MARTHA.** Is this going to help you on the SAT?

**CARL.** It is as useful as anything you are learning at Buck Lodge Junior High. I am going to give you a reading list. And you will read this list in your spare time. It will prepare you for the PSAT.

**MARTHA.** Yeah. Maybe.

**CARL.** You will not be a peasant knocking on the chamber door. You are my sister. And you will go to college.

**MARTHA.** You'll go to college. You'll grow your pinky fingernail long. I'll be in the kitchen plucking the chicken.

**CARL.** The children of rich Washingtonians are going to Sidwell Friends and Washington Cathedral. You are going to match them point for point on the PSATs. What are you reading for fun?

**MARTHA.** Something Mother gave me.

**CARL.** Hand it over.

Jesus Christ. Mother gave you this?

The other lesson is to never read anything Mother gives you.

**MARTHA**. What's wrong with the book?

**CARL**. *The Well of Loneliness* is a depressing autobiographical novel written by an invert.

**MARTHA**. She didn't like people?

**CARL**. No. That's introvert. An invert was the term used for lesbians. Please tell me you know what that term means.

**MARTHA**. *(Blushing, looking down.)* I do. I think.

**CARL**. Edwardians believed that lesbians were men trapped inside women's bodies.

I can't believe Mother gave that book to a fourteen-year-old daughter.

**MARTHA**. Maybe she's warning me.

**CARL**. She's trying to scare you. Into being "normal." Whatever the hell that is.

**MARTHA**. Mother does call me Don Herman Junior.

**CARL**. She needs to leave you alone. But I will tell you this: if I could choose any existence on this earth, I would choose to be a lesbian.

**MARTHA**. Why?

**CARL**. Because. Men are brought up to be competitive. Women are brought up to be nurturers. So when you have two men together, they have to undo their training. But with two women –

**MARTHA**. They take care of each other?

**CARL**. Exactly.

**MARTHA**. Think I'll finish *The Well of Loneliness*, though.

**CARL**. The ending made me suicidal. As did Miss Hellman's *The Children's Hour*.

(**CARL** *cocks his fingers as a gun and shoots himself.*)

Now: about Virginia Woolf and the Bloomsbury Group. I would suggest reading *A Room of One's Own*.

(*They are both startled by the figure of* **PHYLLIS***: half asleep, groggy, thick-tongued.*)

**MARTHA**. Mother?

**PHYLLIS**. Thirsty.

(**PHYLLIS** *goes to the refrigerator. Gets a glass. A spotlight suddenly shines on the counter:* **PHYLLIS** *sees a couple of roaches and tries to smash them with her hand. They are too quick. She beats with both hands and gets at least one. Spotlight out. Then she takes the gin from the freezer and shuffles off to bed with the bottle.*)

## Erie Street, Later

(**PHYLLIS** *in full glory in her house coat is on the phone.*)

### I.

Oh, hello Mr. Montgomery! And how are you today? I realize you are a busy busy man, so I will get to the point: This is Phyllis Herman, and we live at 2109 Erie Street, in the custodial apartment.

My son has been taking out the trash every Wednesday morning, but...we seem to have an infestation.

Vinegar? Mr. Montgomery, our agreement was that we would take the trash out, not that we would clean the garbage room...

**PHYLLIS**. I am also beginning to smell it through our door. May I suggest you come over and smell it for yourself? I see. You will send someone to smell it for you? Thank you, Mr. Montgomery!

*(A change in posture and lighting:)*

## II.

Mr. Montgomery, please. This is Phyllis Herman. Will you please tell him I called?

*(A change in posture and lighting:)*

## III.

Hello. Theresa, yes? Mr. Montgomery never called me back. Oh, a family emergency? Well, then, might you help me, Theresa?

The infestation has Not Abated. There are maggots, and roaches, and I believe I saw a rat.

Maggots and roaches and rats Oh My! We need an exterminator.

As soon as possible.

*(Another change:)*

## IV.

Theresa, my children's asthma and allergies are being exacerbated by rodents and vermin. Ex-Ac-er-Bate. Rhymes with MASTURBATE – Get a dictionary. And I don't want to hear about another family emergency – by now his entire family must be dead unless Mr. Montgomery procreates – Fucks! Like a rabbit... I'm vulgar? You know what vulgar is? Come turn on the lights in my kitchen at night and I'll show you what vulgar is, what filth is, what fucking squalor –

*(Theresa hangs up on the other end of the call.)*

## Next

**PHYLLIS**. Children!

*(They enter. **PHYLLIS** gives **CARL** and **MARTHA** paper towels.)*

Okay children. I want you each to crush at least ten to twenty roaches. Bring me the roach carcasses.

**CARL**. Mother. That's disgusting.

**PHYLLIS**. A dime a roach.

**MARTHA**. Okay!

*(She starts the hunt. We hear the sounds of whacking. Small mini spotlights zig zag on the walls and shelves and furniture.)*

**CARL**. I refuse.

**PHYLLIS**. Fine. The kitchen is mine.

*(Whack. Whack. Whack. Spotlights out. **MARTHA** comes back gingerly holding a stash of smashed roaches. **PHYLLIS** brings in her trophies too. **PHYLLIS** counts. Opens her wallet and takes out two dollars.)*

Excellent job, Martha. Martha, you have balls twice the size of your brother's. And now it is time to pay the rent.

*(**PHYLLIS** takes out her checkbook, and a pen. She puts the check carefully into the envelope. Addresses it. Finds a stamp in her purse and licks it and presses it on the envelope.)*

Martha...put your bounty in this envelope. In back of the check.

*(**PHYLLIS** puts the contents of her paper towel in the envelope.)*

**PHYLLIS.**  Do you know how wonderful technology is, children? Starting tomorrow, the Postal Service will employ mechanical sorting for all first-class mail – Every envelope – like this one, for example – will be run through a machine that will stamp a cancellation code on the envelope between two flat sheets of metal like so:

> (**PHYLLIS** *smashes the envelope between both hands.*)

Presto!

**CARL.**  Wait – so you mean –

**PHYLLIS.**  In mother's house, Revenge is next to godliness. To endorse the check, Mr. Montgomery will have to write his John Hancock on top of the smashed carcasses of roaches found on his slumlord premises –

**CARL.**  Wait!

> (**CARL** *leaps up, finds a roach, and whacks it with his book. He brings the book to* **PHYLLIS***, and she scrapes it off with her nail into the envelope.*)

Killed by Jane Austen.

**MARTHA.**  EVICTION NUMBER ONE

> (*There is a Roach Ballet/dance as the Hermans change residence: think Nicholas Brothers. Upbeat, and Roaches do feats of tap dancing!*)

> (**CARL** *and* **MARTHA** *rearrange the furniture.*)

WILLOWBROOK APARTMENTS. LANGLEY PARK MARYLAND. GROUND FLOOR.

> (*We are now in a ground floor apartment with a slider. Still next to the garbage room. Everything fits. A few boxes.* **PHYLLIS** *glides in.*)

**PHYLLIS.** Ground floor! We are moving up in the world!

**MARTHA.** We are still next to the trash room.

**PHYLLIS.** Well, thanks to my promotion out of the typing pool, we do not have to extract the trash.

**MARTHA.** I'm still sleeping in your room.

**CARL.** I have a companion in my room every night of the week. This week I am lying with Lytton Strachey –

**PHYLLIS.** I could care less who you are sleeping with. Just don't get her pregnant.

**CARL.** Him. It's a he. Don't get Him pregnant. Lytton Strachey was a member of the Bloomsbury group – who were some of their members –

**MARTHA.** – Leonard Woolf /…

**PHYLLIS.** / How is this going to help you in life? Unpack while you are pontificating…

>   (**MARTHA** *opens a box, and rifles into it; there is the tinkling sound of something delicate broken.* **MARTHA** *looks scared.*)

**MARTHA.** Mama! One of the cups broke in the move –

>   (**PHYLLIS** *rushes in.*)

**PHYLLIS.** – Oh. Grandmother Valdez's chocolate cup. Who packed this box?

**MARTHA.** You did.

>   (**PHYLLIS** *takes a closer look.*)

**PHYLLIS.** This cup came all the way from Spain, my children. 1880 something.

Never sell these cups. They are worth some–

FUCK!!!

(**PHYLLIS** *has stopped in horror: a roach climbing up the wall in a spotlight. After all, it lives there. It's fast. It takes three thwacks from* **MARTHA** *to meet its demise.*)

**MARTHA**.  EVICTION NUMBER TWO

(*As the Roaches dance and celebrate their victory by romancing Lady Roaches: a medley of ballroom dancing. Roaches in wedding attire, and then hundreds of their Roach Children come in and dance.* **CARL** *and* **MARTHA** *rearrange the furniture.*)

MARYLAND FARMS, BELTSVILLE, MARYLAND. 1967. A THREE BEDROOM APARTMENT!

(*When full light comes up, we see only* **MARTHA** *onstage.*)

Mama! Carl! We are going to be late for the National Honors Society!

(**CARL** *enters in blue jeans, no belt, a t-shirt, and his flannel shirt open and untucked, wearing sneakers.*)

Jesus. You are really pushing it. You just got suspended for the dress code and you are wearing this for your induction ceremony? The memo they sent home said no denim, no flannel, no decals –

**CARL**.  Miss Dorothy Combe will hopefully implode from rage. She pushed me against a wall and rubbed my sideburns with her finger. "Shave it!"

And I responded to her manhandling as a gentleman does: "Madam, do I tell you when to shave under your arms?"

**MARTHA**.  Just remember after you've left for college, I still have to walk through the halls.

Mama! We are running late.

**CARL.**  Martha, I have to tell someone. I had sex last night.

(**MARTHA** *stares at* **CARL** *as:*)

**PHYLLIS.**  Ta da!

(**PHYLLIS** *appears and stuns her* **CHILDREN***: she is dressed in a denim pants suit. There is a large peace symbol on her back. She wears high-heeled open-toed sandals, exposing her bright red toenails matching her bright red fingernails. Mascara, foundation, and bright red lipstick.*)

**MARTHA.**  Mama. You look –

**CARL.**  – Sensational. Mama, may I escort you?

(*He holds his arm out to hook her arm in his.* **PHYLLIS** *elegantly accepts.* **MARTHA** *opens the door: and they sweep out.*)

**MARTHA.**  FOUR HOURS LATER

(**PHYLLIS** *sweeps in in triumph.*)

**CARL.**  That was splendid! Mama, you got a standing ovation.

**MARTHA.**  Mama, when you stood up in the auditorium today, and flashed the peace sign (**PHYLLIS** *does so.*) my girlfriends turned to me and said "your mother is cool."

(**PHYLLIS** *sits and takes out her cigarettes.* **CARL** *comes over to light her cigarette.*)

**CARL.**  Mama, may I give you a light?

**PHYLLIS.**  Thanks, love.

Martha, dear – a martini? With not too much ice.

**MARTHA.**  MARTINI NUMBER ONE

*(Jump cut:)*

**PHYLLIS**.  Well, I suppose being tossed out of school due to the dress code runs in your genes, Carl darling. That little prissy teacher got me expelled for wearing silk stockings to school!

**CARL**.  I thought you got expelled because you –

**PHYLLIS**.  – Because I wore the silk stockings Sonny got me. Who's telling this story?

Martha dear – *(Holds up her empty glass.)* – not as much vermouth –

*(Another martini materializes.)*

**MARTHA**.  MARTINI NUMBER TWO

*(Jump cut:)*

**PHYLLIS**.  So I thought, screw algebra! World War II was winding down and any able-bodied girl could get a job. And these jobs! Dance all night and be at your desk at eight a.m. Working for the British Embassy, the Navy Department, and finally the premiere advertising agency...where I met your father. I was the receptionist.

Your father came in every week to check on his application or so I thought. Turns out he was checking me out. Jesus, he could charm the skirt off Eleanor Roosevelt. Your father skipped meals to buy me flowers, stockings, Arpège.

But I refused to go out with him for two years. I only dated sailors, soldiers and marines. I considered it my patriotic duty.

**CARL**.  They also serve who only drink and jitterbug.

**PHYLLIS**.  Speaking of drinking – not as much ice, Martha dear –

*(The **SIBLINGS** exchange glances.)*

**CARL.** It's a weekend.

*(Another martini materializes.)*

**MARTHA.** MARTINI NUMBER THREE

*(Jump cut:)*

**PHYLLIS.** – That son of a bitch your father followed me onto the dance floor! He tried to cut in and my date knocked his glasses off. His lens shattered, and so I steered him out to the pier – both of us four sheets to the wind – he was quoting Kierkegaard and some German Poet I'd never heard of – and told me if I didn't marry him he would drown himself. And then he jumped into the Chesapeake.

He waded into deep water, yelling out, "I can't swim!"

**CARL.** Now that's a pickup line!

**PHYLLIS.** Some man on the pier turned to me and said – "Lady, he means it. You'd better call him back."

Found out after we married that he was swimming at Coney Island when he was a boy.

**MARTHA.** It's kind of romantic.

**PHYLLIS.** Martha, dear, make yourself useful:

*(**PHYLLIS** holds up the empty glass.)*

**CARL.** I think the bar is closed.

*(**PHYLLIS** draws out a small gin bottle from her purse.)*

**PHYLLIS.** Well, Martha, at least give your old mother some ice...

**MARTHA.** NUMBER FOUR

*(Jump cut:)*

**PHYLLIS**.  Your dad said: "I've got a rubber. Don't worry. When your father pulled out of me, I found out that in his haste, he had shredded the condom he'd found in the bar. Or knowing him, he just picked the condom up in the parking lot...

(**CARL** *and* **MARTHA** *shiver in repulsion.*)

But oh my god, his passion for me! It was overwhelming. I felt loved – I was loved. I was adored. Hell, I was worshipped.

(**PHYLLIS** *sings a snippet from a musical torch song.*)

(**CARL** *stares at her.*)

– What? What! Well, at least I got married. Carl will never marry. He's too selfish. It's up to Martha to marry. Martha is unremarkable. She is to find an unremarkable man who doesn't have enough imagination to cheat and drink and whore himself around town like her father does. After a year of learning how to cook, Martha will get a bun in the oven, and give me a grandchild. Because, honey, you are never a true woman until you have children.

**MARTHA**.  (*To* **CARL**.) That's okay. I'm not listening. I'm happy to make cocktails, and light cigarettes. And when I leave the room, she won't notice. Because she never noticed me being there in the first place.

NUMBER FIVE – straight from the bottle.

(**MARTHA** *leaves the room.*)

(*Jump cut:*)

**CARL**.  You have got to stop thrusting your ideas of our future and our destinies on us, Mother: your children are going to move beyond the Beltways. Martha doesn't need your encouragement, because she has me.

**PHYLLIS.** You can encourage your sister all you want. But it's a Man's World, my darlings.

**CARL.** Jesus. She is not staying here to fritter away her life to your low expectations.

**PHYLLIS.** Stop giving her books like – who is that lesbian?

**CARL.** Oh for God's sake. Betty Friedan. A highly respected Marxist.

**PHYLLIS.** And Simone de de –

**CARL.** – Beauvoir

**PHYLLIS.** And Gloria what's her name

**CARL.** Steinem. These women are highly intelligent /

**PHYLLIS.** Highly frigid /

**CARL.** Highly articulate /

**PHYLLIS.** Dykes! You know what my mother taught me? You can tell a woman's education by the condition of her floors. The filthier the floors, the higher her degrees…!

Martha, I need more – *(She holds her glass up and turns.)* Martha?

**CARL.** She left the room a while ago. You are too absorbed in your gin to notice.

And I, my dear mother, am wasting my breath on you after the third martini.

> **(PHYLLIS** *puts her head into her hands and sobs.)*

– Mama?

**PHYLLIS.** I threw away my life when I married a goddamn pathological liar! Whose every word was a fucking lie! From "I love you, I'll kill myself" to "I was at work late! She's my secretary!"

**PHYLLIS.** – spending his paycheck on his whores! – And me walking around on fucking egg shells and at the slightest wrong word – wham! A broken nose! Slam! A black eye! And no one – no one stepping in to help me.

**CARL.** Mama – mama – I know. I saw. I wanted to to to… do something.

**PHYLLIS.** He would have beaten the shit out of you too.

**CARL.** I prayed so often: God, make me a Six-Foot-Tall Man.

*(He sits beside her, taking her hand into his.)*

There are good men out there. Somewhere.

**PHYLLIS.** If I'm harsh on your sister, it's because I don't want this to happen to her.

**CARL.** I know.

May I escort you to your boudoir?

**PHYLLIS.** Don't think I can stand right now.

**CARL.** I got you. Upsy daisy!

*(**PHYLLIS** leans on **CARL**; together they struggle across the floor.)*

**PHYLLIS.** You know, I think in a past life you were my husband.

**CARL.** Time to sleep.

*(**CARL** escorts **PHYLLIS** to her bedroom.)*

**MARTHA.** A FAREWELL. 1968. MARTHA, 16. CARL, 18.

*(**CARL**, with a backpack, says goodbye to a tearful **MARTHA**.)*

**CARL.** Don't cry.

**MARTHA.** I'm just so…proud of you. Johns Hopkins.

**CARL.**  We will write each other once a week. And once I'm settled, you can take the bus up.

**MARTHA.**  I'm going to miss you...

**CARL.**  I'll be back. Now: *(He takes something out of his backpack.)* I want you to read these brochures...there will be a quiz when I come back.

**MARTHA.**  I can't get into these schools!

**CARL.**  Yes you can. You are the second most brilliant mind in this household.

**MARTHA.**  No. Mother's right. I'm going to type my way as a temp to pay the University of Maryland tuition.

**CARL.**  Okay. You need to listen. You can get a scholarship. We live below the poverty line, and there's money if you get into these three schools. Now listen: Mother is waiting in the car and you know how she hates to wait.

**MARTHA.**  What's the poverty line mean?

**CARL.**  I want you to stay out of this house as much as you can. Take after school programs.

Volunteer. Go out for school plays. Stay out of the house.

*(***MARTHA*** nods.)*

Promise?

**MARTHA.**  Promise.

**CARL.**  Make sure to keep your floors filthy.

**MARTHA.**  THANKSGIVING 1968. EVICTION NUMBER THREE.

*(A tearful ***MARTHA*** confronts her ***MOTHER*** in the living room.)*

**PHYLLIS.**  You have five minutes to pack up and get out.

**MARTHA.**  Mama! Don't do this!!

**PHYLLIS.**  Well, Martha, we do not need a three-bedroom apartment any longer.

**MARTHA.**  Can we please just discuss this in the morning.

**PHYLLIS.**  No, I am not letting him stay under the same roof as my teenage daughter.

>  (**CARL** *enters with his hair long, dressed like an SDS member and recruit to the Gay Activists Alliance. He carries a grocery bag of hastily packed items.*)

Give me back the key to the apartment. Now.

>  (**CARL** *takes the key off his key ring. He drops the key into the palm of* **PHYLLIS**' *hand.*)

I don't trust you. I'm changing the locks so you can't sneak in when I'm at work.

Look at you. Dressed like some dirty hippy. I can't take you to your grandparents' house looking like that… It's bad enough to bring your counter-cultural crap home…

– but no, you had to bring home your Filthy lifestyle –

**CARL.**  Mother! There's nothing filthy about – loving men. Mama, you've known this all my life.

**PHYLLIS.**  Never in my wildest dreams did I imagine my son is a faggot.

**CARL.**  (*To* **MARTHA.**) There's nothing wrong about how I feel. It's beautiful. It's sacred…

**PHYLLIS.**  And that's another thing. You are to stay away from my daughter. You are not to write each other. I will throw out any of your letters in the trash.

>  (*She rounds on* **MARTHA** *who is crying.*)

You are not to call your brother. I will look at my phone bill every month, and there will be consequences.

**CARL**.  Mama – I thought you'd be happy for me –

**PHYLLIS**.  Happy for you?! That you go down to the Greyhound Bus station and into the bathroom to blow men in the stalls? That is not happiness – that's filth!

I am telling your grandparents that you couldn't come home. You have the flu. Martha, I will beat you to an inch of your life if you tell my parents.

As long as you live under my roof, you are not to see or speak to your brother.

Once upon a time, I had a son… I have no son.

> (**PHYLLIS** *leaves the room. Her* **CHILDREN** *stare at each other.*)

**MARTHA**.  Carl –

**CARL**.  *(Weeping.)* I am Anastasia. The soldier led me to a small basement, and he was scared. He raised his rifle, and asked me to turn my head. I looked into his eyes. He had been a peasant, and his hands were rough. His hands were shaking.

And I asked him for a favor: "I don't want to leave this earth Before I know the taste of a man." He stood there and I lowered the pants of his uniform. When I put him in my mouth, he trembled even more. He took his arm and hid his eyes behind his sleeve.

And I gently Overcame all his thoughts of revolution with my tongue.

He told me to leave. To run.

And ever since, I make love to men as if my life depended on it. Because it does.

> *(Beat.)*

I swear to you, Martha the love I feel for men is sacred.

> (**PHYLLIS** *storms back into the room.*)

**PHYLLIS.**  You are not to talk to my daughter.

**CARL.**  I'm leaving. I am LEAVING!

> (**CARL** *cries in earnest anger; he runs to the
> door. He slams the door. We can hear him
> running up the stairs, and a strangled cry:)*

(*Offstage.*) You are never going to see me again! For
God's Sake – MAMA!

> (*The two* **WOMEN** *are still.* **MARTHA***'s tears
> are transitioning to a hot silent rage.)*

**MARTHA.**  I don't know what his "lifestyle" means. But
I will cut my arm off before I let my brother feel
unaccepted. There is nothing filthy about my brother.

**PHYLLIS.**  I am doing this for you. When you are older, you
will thank me.

**MARTHA.**  No. I won't.

**PHYLLIS.**  You had the choice. When the judge asked you,
who do you want to live with?

You could have gone with your father. You chose me.

**MARTHA.**  No. I didn't. Carl thought you needed someone
to take care of you. He chose you.

I chose Carl.


## Phyllis On the Phone


**PHYLLIS.**  Hi Mama. I'm just calling you to thank you for
another delicious Thanksgiving.

Uh huh. Well – Martha's just at that sullen teenager
age. I know. She barely said two words.

She's a little tetchy about the election. So it didn't help
for Daddy to keep braying the south will rise again!

*(The two share a laugh; then.)*

I'm sorry too. But when Carl told me he had a fever, I told him to stay at school.

What? Is it that late already? I know, Daddy gets mad if his dinner isn't ready –

Yes, you should probably run! – I am going to heat up the leftovers for me and Martha.

Okay, Mama. Call me when you can – Love – *(The line goes dead.)* – You.

## Transition

*(**MARTHA** stands by the U-Haul box from the beginning.)*

**MARTHA.**  The longest period of my life started that Thanksgiving of 1968. Phyllis in, Carl out. No letters. No phone calls. No performances in my mother's living room.

Finally I escaped to one of the fancy colleges selected by Carl. Where I had enough money for postage stamps and one phone call a week – the luxury of hearing his voice answering mine! Phyllis out, Carl in. After that, we were never apart.

In the middle of our lives, we think life is long. What's a decade of time?

*(**MARTHA** and **CARL** reunite. **PHYLLIS** moves the furniture all by herself.)*

HAMPSHIRE TOWERS. TACOMA PARK. SECOND FLOOR.

*(**MARTHA** comes through the door, carrying a big duffel bag. **PHYLLIS** quietly closes the door. **MARTHA** tosses the duffel down.)*

**MARTHA**.  Wow, Mama, such nice light! And elevators. And a front desk. Moving on up!

(**MARTHA** *looks out the second story window.*)

...are you enjoying the high life?

**PHYLLIS**.  It's quiet. My social life consists of talking to my mother on the phone, and going to their apartment for dinner on Sunday.

I'm not sure...if I want to go to this...this – what is it? Therapy?

**MARTHA**.  It's not therapy. It's a support group. P-FLAG

**PHYLLIS**.  What kind of support?

**MARTHA**.  Well, there are parents of gay children, and there are gay children. And a therapist who is a parent of a gay child.

It might help to talk.

**PHYLLIS**.  There's a therapist?! That is just a waste of money.

**MARTHA**.  Mother – it's free.

**PHYLLIS**.  Oh, it's free? For me to sit there and hear how it's all the mother's fault?

**MARTHA**.  That's a myth. Which we can talk about. There's no proof of any connection between parenting and the sexuality of the offspring.

Just try it. Once. For me. I know you miss your son.

**PHYLLIS**.  I suppose you talk to Carl.

**MARTHA**.  I do. And he misses you.

**PHYLLIS**.  All right. Just one session.

**MARTHA**.  I'm proud of you.

**PHYLLIS**.  Don't tell Daddy and Mama that I'm going to – what's the name?

MARTHA.  PFLAG. It's our secret.

MONTHS LATER, OUTSIDE LOST AND FOUND DISCO

*(The apartment fades into the background.* **MARTHA** *escorts her* **MOTHER.***)*

PHYLLIS.  I don't know.

MARTHA.  Listen, didn't the parents tell you to come? You are making such great progress, Mama! It will change your notion of gays as solitary creatures preying on men in bathrooms.

PHYLLIS.  I don't know this neighborhood. It looks like a place where mothers are murdered.

MARTHA.  It's the Warehouse District. Bars. Little cabarets. And, uh, bars. We're going into the most fabulous dance floor in all of Washington D.C.! Come on, Mama. It will be fun. Welcome to Lost and Found!

*(They step into the music and the lights of Lost and Found. Across the room is* **CARL.***)*

PHYLLIS.  *(Starts to cry.)* There he is. Carl!

*(***CARL** *comes across to them somewhat tentatively.)*

CARL.  Mama. You look wonderful. Chanel?

PHYLLIS.  Von Furstenberg. You have to be au courant, son.

MARTHA.  What do you think?

PHYLLIS.  It's...nice in here.

MARTHA.  Men dancing with men, women dancing with women, and quite a few men dancing with women.

CARL.  Mama – would you care to dance?

> (**PHYLLIS** *awkwardly steps forward with her* **SON**. *She is not used to solo dancing. But she is pretty damn good at it. A 1970s disco song is playing. They dance for a while.* **PHYLLIS** *spins. She is starting to enjoy herself when she stops.*)

> (**PHYLLIS** *quotes an inane lyric from the song.*)

**PHYLLIS**.  What the hell?

**CARL**.  Never to listen to the lyrics in a dance palace. Like Mairzy Doats and and dozey doats and little lambs eat –

**PHYLLIS**.  – Shut up and dance with me son.

> (**PHYLLIS** *leads her* **SON** *in dancing to the finale of a beloved 1970s disco tune – strange lyrics are a plus. They go back to* **MARTHA**, *who is grinning as the intro to another disco anthem starts.*)

Okay, daughter, dear. Your turn.

**MARTHA**.  Oh, I don't dance, Mama.

**PHYLLIS**.  The night is young –

> (**PHYLLIS** *pulls* **MARTHA** *onto the dance floor.* **PHYLLIS** *camps it up, taking her scarf off and waving it – then she takes* **MARTHA** *in her arms.*)

That's it. Loosen up, girl. Come on! Follow what Mama does…

> (*She pulls* **MARTHA**'s *arms around her back, and leads forward in a strange Conga line.* **CARL** *joins behind* **MARTHA**. *The three of them crack up with laughter.*)

**MARTHA.** Excuse me. I need to go powder my nose. Do you wanna come with me, Mama?

**PHYLLIS.** Go to the ladies' room in a gay bar? I'll hold it, thanks.

(**MARTHA** *makes her way offstage.*)

**CARL.** I hope you're having a good time tonight.

**PHYLLIS.** It is so much nicer than I imagined! – Is that a cowboy?

**CARL.** Where?

**PHYLLIS.** The man wearing the leather chaps...

**CARL.** That's Herbert. He's an accountant –

**PHYLLIS.** His ass is hanging out the back – Oh!

**CARL.** It's not polite to gawk.

(**PHYLLIS** *sees something more distressing.*)

**PHYLLIS.** *(All levity has gone.)* Who Is That Woman??! Kissing your sister?

(**CARL** *turns around.*)

**CARL.** (oh crap.) It's just some friend. Of Martha's –

**PHYLLIS.** What *kind* of friend.

**CARL.** I don't know her.

**PHYLLIS.** The evening is ruined. You both have made an idiot of me. As usual.

**CARL.** Mother, you are jumping to conclusions.

**PHYLLIS.** I could see that woman's tongue down your sister's throat from here.

(**PHYLLIS** *breaks away, goes outside for air.*)

I'm going to be sick.

(**PHYLLIS** *lowers her head towards the ground.*)

**CARL**.  Mama –

(**MARTHA** *has joined them.*)

**MARTHA**.  What's wrong?

**CARL**.  She saw your friend kiss you.

**PHYLLIS**.  Was it too much to ask for one normal child?

**MARTHA**.  I was going to tell you...at next month's PFLAG.

**PHYLLIS**.  You are never going to find the acceptance you want in this world as a lesbian.

**MARTHA**.  So be it, Mama. I can't suppress what I feel.

And you are repulsed by women. We are scared to touch each other /

**PHYLLIS**.  / Who just asked you to dance /?

**MARTHA**.  / You can't blame me if I need to be touched. I don't want to end up like you,

Calling your mother everyday –

**CARL**.  – Can we not have this discussion in / public?

**PHYLLIS**.  / That's right! Blame the mother!

**MARTHA**.  I am not like Carl. Gay sons and mothers! The first question he asks me when we call each other is "How is Mother?" Gay men carry a lifelong guilt because their little heads popped out of their mother's vagina, which they think is sacred. Or some such bullshit.

**CARL**.  Martha – this isn't helping.

**MARTHA**.  But I have a vagina just like you.

**PHYLLIS**.  Tomorrow you can drop by and pick up your lesbian army-navy duffle bag. It will be in the hallway.

**MARTHA**. Carl will come running back when you call him. I won't.

**PHYLLIS**. Jesus Christ! Two of them.

(**PHYLLIS** *leaves. Beat.*)

**CARL**. Sweetie. I'll make up the sofa for you in my place.

**MARTHA**. EVICTION NUMBER FOUR

(*The lights fade back into the apartment lights.*)

## The Phyllis Ballet

(*The following is a suggestion. The actor and director should adjust to the production.*)

(*To a medley of soft and easy music, Phyllis comes home from work. Throws keys and wallet on the table. Stands a moment. Looks through the mail. Bills. Ads. Puts bills into a tidy pile. Walks to the lounger. She sits. Takes off her heels. Massages her stocking feet. Pause. She listens to the silence. Takes off her wig. [Productions may choose not to have a wig.] Scratches her head. Ahh. Runs her hand through what remains of her hair. Stands. Exits to the bedroom with shoes and wig. Comes back in a flamboyant, expensive silk dressing robe. Only ten dollars! Looks around the living room. Turns off the radio. Turns on the television. Sits. Lights up a cigarette. Watches TV without interest. Clucks in dismay. Looks at her watch. Slowly takes off her stockings. Sits a moment. Brings the crotch of her stockings to her nose. Considers.*

*Yes, she can still wear them tomorrow. Gently starts to fold the stockings. She sees a run. She holds the stockings up, inserts her hand down the legs, scrutinizes the run. Puts the stockings down. Exits. Enters with fingernail polish. Carefully opens polish, finds the run, and slathers the polish on the run. Blows the hosiery. Inspects. One more day?)*

*(She inspects one more time... Damn. Another run. She wads the stockings up to discard. Leaves the living room. Comes back in with a wig stand. White Styrofoam face with lipstick that Phyllis put on as a joke. She mounts her wig on the stand. Examines. Exits, and reenters with combs and hair spray. Looks at her watch. Not yet. Phyllis wills herself to wait until five p.m. for the first drink. Keep busy, Phyllis. Phyllis does a comb out on her own "hair." She swivels it around and combs and sprays from each angle. Satisfied, she then takes a big puff of her cigarette. And then pours on the spray. She picks up the mannequin wig stand.)*

*(Phyllis goes offstage. We can hear the refrigerator open, the clank of ice, and she appears with her first martini with great anticipation. She sits elegantly, and lifts her glass as if being toasted by a single, attractive, available date. Nods. Sips. Sighs.)*

*(Relaxes. Turns on the radio again and allows herself to sink into her music. Rodgers and Hammerstein, Porter, Gershwin, a sprinkle of hits. By the end of the song, she has finished her drink. She looks down and swivels the cubes. She looks at her watch.)*

*(Wait, Phyllis. She sits stock still, emotiveless.)*

*(She sits for far longer than we are used to watching people sit.)*

*(The she gets up, empty glass in hand. Puts down the glass, and brings both hands to her scalp, and really tunnels her hand into her own hair. Ahhhh.)*

*(Then she picks up the glass, and exits into the kitchen. We hear the freezer opened, and then we hear a microwave; Phyllis comes out with a little TV tray that she opens in front of her chair. Exits. She comes back in with a cloth napkin, utensils. She carefully sets her dinner tray. Wait. She exits and comes back in with a small vase and a single flower. Nods in satisfaction.)*

*(She hears the microwave beep. Goes back into the kitchen. Comes out with her dinner on a plate, holding it with two oven mitts. Puts the dinner on the tray, and exits.)*

*(She comes back in and seats herself, a bit formally, as if someone is holding her chair out. She puts the napkin on her lap with some flair. She wishes an imaginary dinner companion a "bon appetit" with an imaginary wine glass.)*

*(She lifts a forkful of food. Tests the temperature. Hot. Picks it up again and blows on it. Then she tastes it critically. Not too bad. Missing something. She stands and comes back with Tabasco and liberally shakes it on her food. Puts the Tabasco down. Tastes. It's okay. Maybe she's losing her taste buds.)*

*(She dutifully puts another forkful in her mouth, and chews thoughtfully. Then another when – she douses it with Tabasco. Tastes it, spits it out.)*

*(She looks at her watch. Goes into the kitchen, comes back with a full glass of gin and a sprinkle of vermouth. Sits. Savors her drink. Eats a little more. Then realizes she has had enough food to titrate the alcohol. Fuck it. She puts her fork down and lights up another cigarette.)*

*(The silence is growing beneath the easy muzak. She can hear it creeping below the swelling strings. Another sip. Another drag. The pleasures of the flesh, ahhh. She sits still and listens to the next song. She lets the memories of Sonny or Bernie or the other boys in uniform overtake her, the last moments of adolescence before she got knocked up. She brings herself into the present moment. Slugs down the rest of the gin now, the way one does in the privacy of your living room. She takes the rest of her cigarette and stubs it out in her food. Rises. Stretches. Buses her tray offstage.)*

*(Turns off the music. She looks intently around the living room. Comes back in with a crystal ball.)*

*(The crystal ball has one of her scarves wrapped on top of it...a next to new scarf for three dollars. She sits. Unveils the crystal ball. Then tries to channel the energy, her eyes closed. She sits and inhales. Exhales. Uses her hand to wave the energy around her into being a conduit.)*

**PHYLLIS**.  Um...ohm...ohm... O Crystal ball, make my husband's second wife grow thick facial hair... *(She cracks herself up.)*

*(Second try. **PHYLLIS** settles. Stares into the ball. Ohms. Ohms. She thinks she sees something.)*

*(She sits forward intent now, and stares. Whatever she sees is deeply unsettling.)*

**MARTHA**.  1982. MARTHA, 30. CARL 32. PHYLLIS 55.

*(**CARL** and **MARTHA** unpack food from a grocery bag. **MARTHA** finds three glasses, and **CARL** takes out the gin from the freezer.)*

*(They wear their Sunday best funeral clothes.)*

**CARL**.  How does she seem to you?

**MARTHA**.  I expected more keening. More performance.

**CARL**.  She's lost the only person in the world who listened to her.

**MARTHA**.  The apartment...is just the same. Nothing has changed –

*(**MARTHA** sees the crystal ball.)*

– What the hell is that?!

**CARL**.  Don't make fun of her. Martha. Mama's gone a little around the bend – tarot cards and crystal balls.

*(**PHYLLIS** enters in black.)*

Sit down here, Mama. Put your feet up.

*(He leads **PHYLLIS** to the sofa.)*

**MARTHA**.  Eat something, Mother?

**PHYLLIS.**  I called my mother every day. Every single day.

**MARTHA.**  I used to fantasize that Grandma would have a decade or so after her husband died: to put her feet up, to do as she liked…but Jesus, to die the next day after him!?

**PHYLLIS.**  Did it ever occur to you that my mother loved my father?

The two of them in their caskets, side by side. It was like an engagement party in that chapel!

**MARTHA.**  Complete with a priest who couldn't remember their names.

**PHYLLIS.**  There will be no priests at my graveside. Buggers in robes. Fucking Catholic Church.

**CARL.**  Excuse me, Mama. I need to powder my nose.

(**CARL** *leaves.*)

**PHYLLIS.**  You've gained weight.

**MARTHA.**  And you have not.

**PHYLLIS.**  I've been practicing meditation with a crystal ball. I can tell you, my girl, that there is so much we don't understand. Don't laugh… I've seen things…

**MARTHA.**  I'm not laughing.

**PHYLLIS.**  I would tell you what I see about your brother's future but – it's too terrible.

**MARTHA.**  For God's sake, Mother! Do not say a word. Not a word.

(**CARL** *reenters.*)

**PHYLLIS.**  This is the time of day when I would call Mama.

**CARL.**  It's going to be hard. May I suggest we all have a little gin and salute them both?

**MARTHA.**  Got it.

(**MARTHA** *apportions the gin – one to* **PHYLLIS**, *one to* **CARL**, *and a big one for her.*)

**CARL.**  To Vera and Benjamin.

**PHYLLIS.**  The best parents a girl could ask for.

(**MARTHA** *gives a slight eye roll, and* **CARL** *admonishes her silently.*)

(*A beat of silence.* **CARL** *and* **PHYLLIS** *sip;* **MARTHA** *slugs hers.*)

**CARL.**  The apartment still looks lovely, Mama.

**PHYLLIS.**  The building is going to shit. Soon I'll be the only one in the lobby speaking English.

**MARTHA.**  Whatever hideous racist jokes your father told you, please don't repeat in front of me.

**PHYLLIS.**  I'm sorry, I won't offend your liberal sensibilities.

It's hard for me – the way I've been brought up – but I am going to try to be more accepting of your...your...

**MARTHA.**  Lifestyles?

**PHYLLIS.**  Yes. And maybe in time I can meet your...your...

**CARL.**  Our partners.

**PHYLLIS.**  Your roommates.

**MARTHA.**  You mean our lovers.

**PHYLLIS.**  I just ask that you don't push it in my face.

**MARTHA.**  You mean you don't want me to tell you the details of what we do in bed together?

**CARL.**  Martha – please don't gnaw on the olive branch.

**PHYLLIS.**  My parents are, were the last of the depression age. Paying bills on time. No credit cards. Making casseroles of the leftovers. Pinching pennies. And I'm their daughter.

**CARL.**  It's time for you to spend money on yourself, Mama.

**PHYLLIS.**  If we have time this week – maybe we could go look at condos.

>*(**PHYLLIS** pats the sofa beside her.)*

Come sit with me, Martha.

>*(**CARL** sits on one side; **MARTHA** carefully sits on the other. **PHYLLIS** flings her arm around **CARL,** and awkwardly pats **MARTHA**'s knee. The two **WOMEN** look at each other. **PHYLLIS** takes **MARTHA**'s hand in hers:)*

It's going to be a new age in the Herman family.

## Transition

>*(**CARL** and **MARTHA** and **PHYLLIS** rearrange the furniture. The stage is flooded with light. The living room in the new apartment is larger than the previous apartments.)*

>*(Once the stage empties of people, one of the unpacked boxes slowly flaps open:)*

>*(Two adult Roaches from the last apartment carefully come out, and with antennae twitching, ascertain that the coast is clear; a roach signal, and several smaller Roaches come out of the box.)*

**MARTHA.**  LEISURE WORLD. THREE YEARS LATER. FIFTH FLOOR.

>*(**PHYLLIS,** almost giddy, enters carrying her crystal ball. **CARL** exits to the bathroom.)*

**PHYLLIS.**  Can you believe the light in here?!

**MARTHA.**  You can see the golf course from here.

**PHYLLIS.**  I'm going to buy binoculars, sit on the enclosed balcony, and watch the geese and the golfers.

**MARTHA.**  I'm glad for you, Mama.

**PHYLLIS.** This is the American Dream. A Gated Community!

Where is Carl? He's been awfully quiet. Carl? Carl!

**MARTHA.**  Mama. Sit down. I have something hard to tell you.

> (*In mime behind* **MARTHA**, *we see* **PHYLLIS** *crumple in grief, keening.* **CARL** *rushes in. We can see how weak he is becoming.* **PHYLLIS** *wraps her arms around her* **SON**.)

We all know what time it is: the 1980s. And we all knew what was coming. But knowing it's coming and stopping it are different things. In the aftermath the only thing we can do is witness:

**CARL.**  I'm sorry Mama. I'm sorry.

**PHYLLIS.**  I want you to move in with me. I want you to come home.

**CARL.**  Are you sure?

**PHYLLIS.**  I'm your mother.

> (*A sharp change of light:*)

**MARTHA.**  THE LAST EVICTION. 6 MONTHS LATER

> (**MARTHA**, *in her coat, stands in her* **MOTHER**'s *living room.*)

**PHYLLIS.**  Sit down, Martha.

**MARTHA.**  Where's Carl?

**PHYLLIS**.  He's in his room. It's best if we don't share the same living room. Sit down.

   *(***MARTHA*** sits. ***PHYLLIS*** sits.)*

All right. I am not going to win Mother of the Year. So I have something you need to hear. I never wanted to be a mother. I didn't have a choice.

**MARTHA**.  I know.

**PHYLLIS**.  No, you don't know. I couldn't afford a hack abortionist. I was scared to die on someone's kitchen table. My father told me that marrying a Jew was still better than being a whore. Either way I was no longer welcome under his roof. So I bit the bullet. I thought: other women aren't mother material but they get through it. Just hang on, Phyllis, hang on.

But it is never over. It's a life sentence.

**MARTHA**.  I'm sorry you feel that way.

   *(***MARTHA*** looks at her ***MOTHER***.)*

**PHYLLIS**.  I finally move into a gated community and people avoid me in the lobby. An elevator building! And neighbors won't get into the elevator with me – with us… I've spent a lot of time as a prisoner in my bedroom while your brother has invaded my space with his rage. His depression. His remorse.

**MARTHA**.  Carl has nothing to be remorseful for!

**PHYLLIS**.  He fucked away his promise. His talent. His – what do you tell your students? His voice.

And so have I. I've been asking: Phyllis, is this what retirement is going to be? …

I quit! I can't, I can't – I don't think my heart is strong enough. I quit.

**MARTHA**.  Well. *(She stands.)* I'd like to get Carl out of here.

(**PHYLLIS** *exits.*)

Carl?

(**CARL**, *dressed in his coat, comes onstage with a packed suitcase. He can barely move it. His face is covered with Kaposi's lesions.*)

Carl, I'll carry that.

(**CARL** *perches on the suitcase, furious.*)

CARL.  The things that come out of her mouth!! I've told her I have pneumonia and she lights up cigarettes right in front of me.

(**CARL** *tries to stand, and slumps back onto his suitcase.*)

She is discarding me. She called you to take out the trash!

MARTHA.  Okay. It's okay. I'm taking us to a nice hotel. And tomorrow we'll look for an apartment. Do you remember when we spent evenings together in high school? It was almost like playing house. That's what we'll do. We will find an apartment. And four walls to hold us. I'll unpack the furniture and we will make a home together.

(**CARL** *is crying as* **MARTHA** *comforts him.*)

CARL.  I want you to keep her away from me. The last thing I want is to hear her voice, while I am dying, unable to move.

MARTHA.  I don't know if I can ever forgive her.

(*To us.*) My brother never saw his mother again.

CARL GETS HIS OWN CONDOMINIUM. ROCK CREEK VILLAGE 19...

(**MARTHA** *can't say it.*) ...19...

> (**CARL** *comes behind her.*)

> (*Note: The following is the letter my brother,
> Carl S. Vogel, wrote to me in 1987.*)

**CARL.** 1987.

> (*Throughout the following,* **MARTHA** *tries
> to push furniture into Carl's apartment,
> attempting to set up one more apartment.*)

> (*But* **CARL** *pushes the furniture out, clearing
> the space.*)

Dear Martha:

I thought I would jot down some of my thoughts about
the (shall we say) production values of my ceremony.
Oh God – I can hear you groaning – everybody wants
to direct.

Well, I want a good show, even though my role has
been reduced involuntarily from player to prop.

First, concerning the choice between a religious
ceremony and a memorial service. I wish prayers in
some recognizably traditional form to be said, prayers
that give thanks to the Creator for the gift of life and
the hope of reunion. For reasons, which you appreciate,
I prefer a woman cleric to lead the prayers.

As for the piece of me I leave behind, here are your
options:

1. Open casket, full drag.

2. Open casket, bum up (You'll know where to place
the calla lilies, won't you?)

3. Closed casket, interment with the grandparents.

4. Cremation and dispersion of my ashes in some
sylvan spot.

(**MARTHA** *looks, and gasps: there is a large growing crack in the walls, dazzling light begins spilling in.* **MARTHA** *tries to keep the wall together, but the crack grows, and the wall begins to disintegrate or slowly fly away. As* **CARL** *continues, he retreats backwards upstage, and the light becomes brighter.)*

(*As* **CARL** *mentions the pieces of music, they each start to play:)*

I would really like good music. My tastes in these matters run to the highbrow: Fauré's "Pie Jesu" from his Requiem, Gluck's "Dance of the Blessed Spirits" from *Orfeo*, "La Vergine degli Angeli" from Verdi's *Forza*. But my favorite song is "I Dream of Jeanie," and I wouldn't mind a spiritual like "Steal Away." Also, perhaps, "Nearer My God to Thee." Didn't Jeanette MacDonald sing that di-vinely in San Francisco?

Well, my dear, that's that. Should I be laid with Grandma and Papa Ben, do stop by for a visit from year to year. And feel free to chat. You'll find me a good listener.

(*The music stops. The entire apartment has fallen down flat or the back wall has flown away into the sky. Everything is gone except the box that* **MARTHA** *opened at the beginning of the play. She stands reading the end of the letter.)*

**MARTHA.**  Love,

Brother

(**MARTHA** *kneels on the floor, and with a tape dispenser seals the box. She lifts the box and:)*

SERENITY HOUSE. MONTGOMERY COUNTY. THE PRESENT.

*(Easy soft listening music welcomes visitors
but most importantly, sedates residents.)*

*(***MARTHA*** reenters with ***PHYLLIS*** in her
wheelchair.)*

**MARTHA.**  Hi, Mama.

**PHYLLIS.**  I want to go home.

**MARTHA.**  This is home.

**PHYLLIS.**  This is not my home. I want My Home.

**MARTHA.**  Mama, remember what I told you?? We sold
your apartment so we could afford your own room here.
This is the nicest assisted living home in Montgomery
County.

**PHYLLIS.**  Where's Carl?

**MARTHA.**  Carl has left us. He's gone, Mama.

**PHYLLIS.**  Where did he go? I want Carl.

**MARTHA.**  I don't want you to get upset. Carl is dead. A
long time ago.

**PHYLLIS.**  You must be a staff member. Lying to me. Carl
would never leave me in this place.

**MARTHA.**  You like this place!

**PHYLLIS.**  I hate this place.

**MARTHA.**  Oh Mama, the counselor told me you are
making great progress.

**PHYLLIS.**  I'm lonely.

**MARTHA.**  Well, every morning they invite you to do chair
yoga. I wish you would.

*(Beat.)*

**PHYLLIS.**  Who are you?

**MARTHA**.  Mama, it's Martha. I'm your daughter.

(**PHYLLIS** *bursts into laughter.*)

Why is that funny?

**PHYLLIS**.  You are much too old to be Martha! And you are much too old *for* Martha. You are not Martha's type. Martha would never let herself go like you have.

**MARTHA**.  Okay! I've gotten old taking care of you.

**PHYLLIS**.  I want to go home.

I hate it here!

**MARTHA**.  That's too bad. It costs a great deal of money. More than your condo. The cost has wiped out Carl's savings, your savings and soon – do you know I haven't been able to take a vacation for three years because of SERENITY HOUSE? So I want you to enjoy everything here!

**PHYLLIS**.  Why doesn't Carl come to visit? Where is Martha? My kids hate me.

**MARTHA**.  Mama: I am right here.

(**MARTHA** *takes her* **MOTHER**'s *arms and shakes her arms a little too briskly.*)

I Come Every Damn Week!

**PHYLLIS**.  *(Starting to cry.)* I don't remember what I did to my children. Whatever it is, I'm sorry.

**MARTHA**.  Let me get you a Kleenex...

(**MARTHA** *looks in her purse and hands her* **MOTHER** *a Kleenex.* **PHYLLIS** *doesn't take it.* **MARTHA** *wipes her* **MOTHER**'s *face. And then puts the Kleenex in front of her* **MOTHER**'s *nose.)*

Blow.

*(With a slight repulsion, **MARTHA** sops up
the mucus from her **MOTHER**'s nose.)*

**MARTHA.**  That's good.

*(There is a pause. **PHYLLIS** begins to drift off.)*

**PHYLLIS.**  Where's Carl? I want Carl...

*(One of the high back loungers turns around
slowly of its own velocity. The ghost of **CARL**
is sitting in the chair as if he's in his mother's
living room. Reading. But listening to every
word. His face is clear, without a trace of KS.
**MARTHA** feels him there. **PHYLLIS** does not.)*

**MARTHA.**  Carl had to leave. Don't you remember? He left,
blowing you a kiss.

**PHYLLIS.**  He loves me?

**MARTHA.**  Don't be silly. He's your son.

**PHYLLIS.**  Why are you here?

**MARTHA.**  That is the thousand-dollar question. I'm here
because I am your daughter.

**PHYLLIS.**  If you say so.

*(The standard song, Phyllis' favorite, starts
to play in the background.)*

**MARTHA.**  Oh! Mama! Do you remember this? You love
this song.

*(**PHYLLIS** stares at **MARTHA**.)*

**PHYLLIS.**  I want to go home.

*(**MARTHA** loses it.)*

**MARTHA.**  For the last time, Jesus Christ Mama, this is
your home. This is it. End of the line.

Be glad you have a roof over your head. Be glad you don't have a mother kicking you to the curb when you need love and care the most.

**PHYLLIS.** You're mean. (**PHYLLIS** *spies her purse.*) And you're a thief! That's my purse.

**MARTHA.** I took it the day you came to Serenity House. You are not using it anymore. /

**PHYLLIS.** / She's stealing my purse!

**MARTHA.** Your purse is magical – you can carry the kitchen sink in here.

**PHYLLIS.** She is stealing my purse!!

**MARTHA.** All right, visiting hours are over for today!

> (**MARTHA** *turns the wheelchair around, and starts pushing* **PHYLLIS** *offstage.*)

Okay, Bye Mom!

> (**MARTHA** *gives the wheelchair a shove offstage.*)

(*Loudly.*) See you next week!!

> (**MARTHA** *is alone with* **CARL** *reading but also sitting in judgement.*)

(*To* **CARL**.) What.

Don't judge me. I am more than pulling my weight here. You just – You left me holding the bag, my brother.

I'm not coming back. I can't. I owe her nothing.

She wouldn't know if I stayed home and let strangers change her diapers and talk to her and touch her gently...as mothers should be touched. But I can't bear to touch her, and she can't bear to be touched by me.

Thank God at the end I was able to hold you and tell you how much you were loved... even after you had no pulse in case hearing really is the last sense to go.

**MARTHA**.  I felt this ferocious possession to keep you as long as I could. I remember thinking: this is how it feels to be a mother. Everyone needs a mother.

But here I am.

You were so angry at her at the end. I've been holding onto your anger and onto mine...

I want to take our anger and throw it like bread into the sea.

Or better still, bury it in the bottom of her purse; where it will never be found.

Okay. Here we go: I am doing this for us.

> (*She walks to her purse and pulls out the basin. Then* **MARTHA** *wheels her* **MOTHER** *onstage.*)

Hello, Mrs. Herman! I hear it is time for your sponge bath. Would you like that?

**PHYLLIS**.  Oh yes, please. Who are you?

**MARTHA**.  I'm...here to bathe you.

**PHYLLIS**.  You know, you remind me of my daughter.

**MARTHA**.  Oh. I hope that's a nice thing.

> (**MARTHA** *unwraps her* **MOTHER**'s *housedress and slides the fabric off of her shoulders.*)

**PHYLLIS**.  Oh it is. She's so smart. And pretty. And so successful!

> (**MARTHA** *is struck. She stands for a moment.*)

**MARTHA**.  You must be very proud.

**PHYLLIS**.  Oh yes. I'm very lucky.

*(Then* **MARTHA** *tenderly washes her* **MOTHER***'s face. She brushes back her* **MOTHER***'s hair, and washes her* **MOTHER***'s neck.)*

**MARTHA.** How does that feel?

**PHYLLIS.** It feels wonderful. It's so nice to be touched.

*(***MARTHA** *washes her* **MOTHER***'s body.)*

## End of Play

www.ingramcontent.com/pod-product-compliance
Lightning Source LLC
Chambersburg PA
CBHW070649120726
47909CB00004B/1646